Dear Parent:
Your child's love of reading starts here!

Every child learns to read in a different way and at his or her own speed. Some go back and forth between reading levels and read favorite books again and again. Others read through each level in order. You can help your young reader improve and become more confident by encouraging his or her own interests and abilities. From books your child reads with you to the first books he or she reads alone, there are I Can Read Books for every stage of reading:

SHARED READING
Basic language, word repetition, and whimsical illustrations, ideal for sharing with your emergent reader

BEGINNING READING
Short sentences, familiar words, and simple concepts for children eager to read on their own

READING WITH HELP
Engaging stories, longer sentences, and language play for developing readers

READING ALONE
Complex plots, challenging vocabulary, and high-interest topics for the independent reader

ADVANCED READING
Short paragraphs, chapters, and exciting themes for the perfect bridge to chapter books

I Can Read Books have introduced children to the joy of reading since 1957. Featuring award-winning authors and illustrators and a fabulous cast of beloved characters, I Can Read Books set the standard for beginning readers.

A lifetime of discovery begins with the magical words **"I Can Read!"**

Visit www.icanread.com for information
on enriching your child's reading experience.

Spider-Man Versus the Vulture © 2009 Marvel Entertainment, Inc., and its subsidiaries. MARVEL, all related characters and the distinctive likenesses thereof: ™ and © 2009 Marvel Entertainment, Inc., and its subsidiaries. Licensed by Marvel Characters B.V. www.marvel.com. All rights reserved. Printed in the United States of America. No part of this book may be used or reproduced in any manner whatsoever without written permission except in the case of brief quotations embodied in critical articles and reviews. For information address HarperCollins Children's Books, a division of HarperCollins Publishers, 1350 Avenue of the Americas, New York, NY 10019.
www.icanread.com

Library of Congress catalog card number: 2008928092
ISBN 978-0-06-162618-0
Typography by Joe Merkel

1 2 3 4 5 6 7 8 9 10   ❖   First Edition

I Can Read!

READING 2 WITH HELP

THE AMAZING SPIDER-MAN

Spider-Man Versus the Vulture

by Susan Hill
pictures by Andie Tong
colors by Jeremy Roberts

HarperCollins Publishers

PETER PARKER

Peter Parker is a very good student.

FLASH THOMPSON

He goes to school with Flash Thompson.

AUNT MAY

Peter lives with his aunt May.

SPIDER-MAN

Peter has a secret identity.
He is Spider-Man!

MR JAMESON

Peter works for Mr. Jameson
at the *Daily Bugle*.

THE VULTURE

The Vulture is one of
Spider-Man's worst enemies.
Can Spidey stop him from
causing danger?

Brrrrrring! Class was over.

Peter Parker packed up his

magnets and grabbed his jacket.

"What's your hurry, Peter?" the teacher asked.

"Today is my first day at the *Daily Bugle*," said Peter. "I can't be late!"

"Too bad you can't swing on a web like Spider-Man!" said the teacher.

"Ha!" Flash Thompson laughed. "Peter Parker, a Super Hero? He's just a bookworm!"

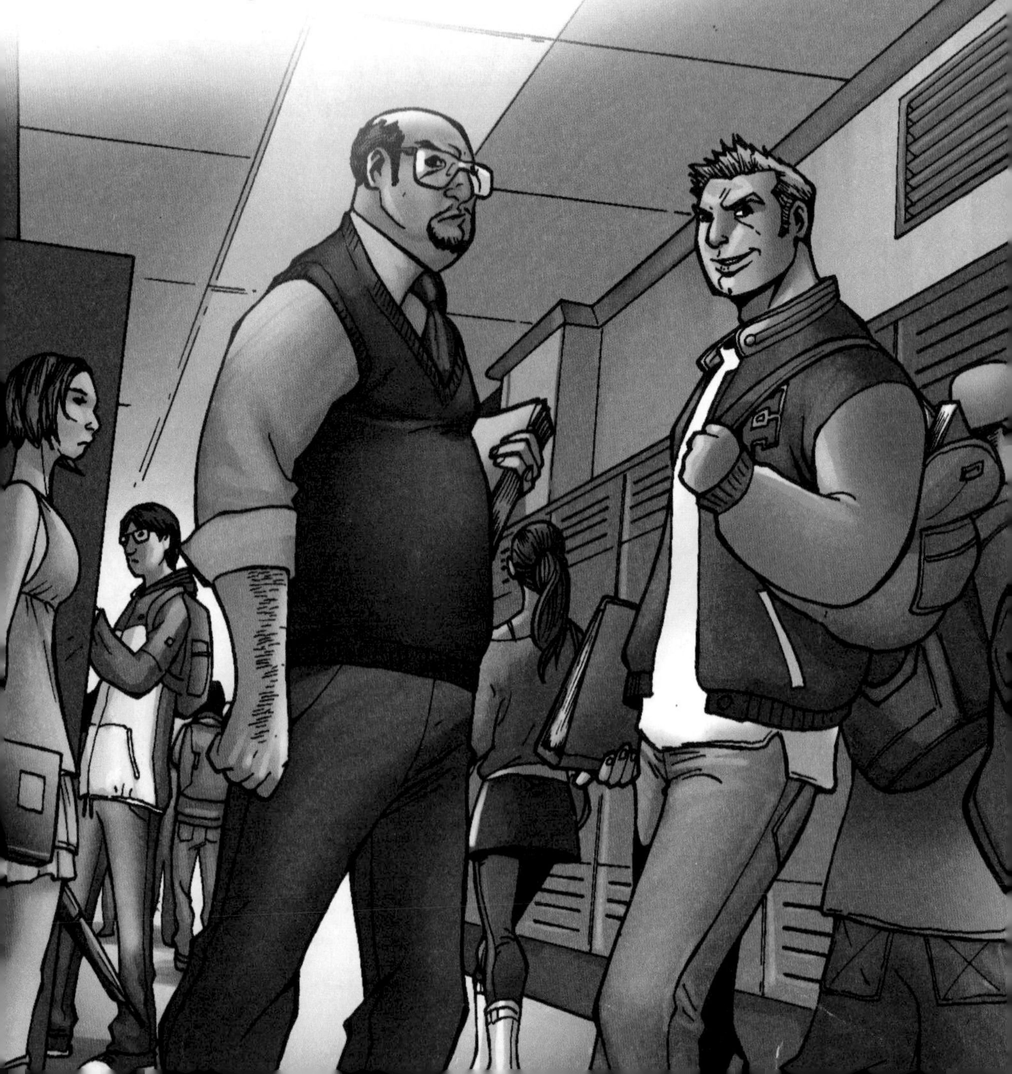

Peter disliked being called names like bookworm, geek, or nerd. "If only he knew my secret. Then I'd show that bully."

Peter was going to be late!

"I know how to get there fast,"

Peter thought.

He ran into an alley

and pulled off his street clothes.

Under Peter's shirt
was a Super Hero costume.
Shy Peter Parker was Spider-Man!

11

Ever since Peter was bitten

by a super-spider,

he has had superpowers!

He has spider-senses.

He has spider-strength.

And he can climb like a spider!

The Vulture appeared from above.

"What's your hurry, Spider-Man?"

The Vulture was a tricky enemy.

He had wings and could fly.

"Vulture! What are you doing here?"
said Spider-Man.

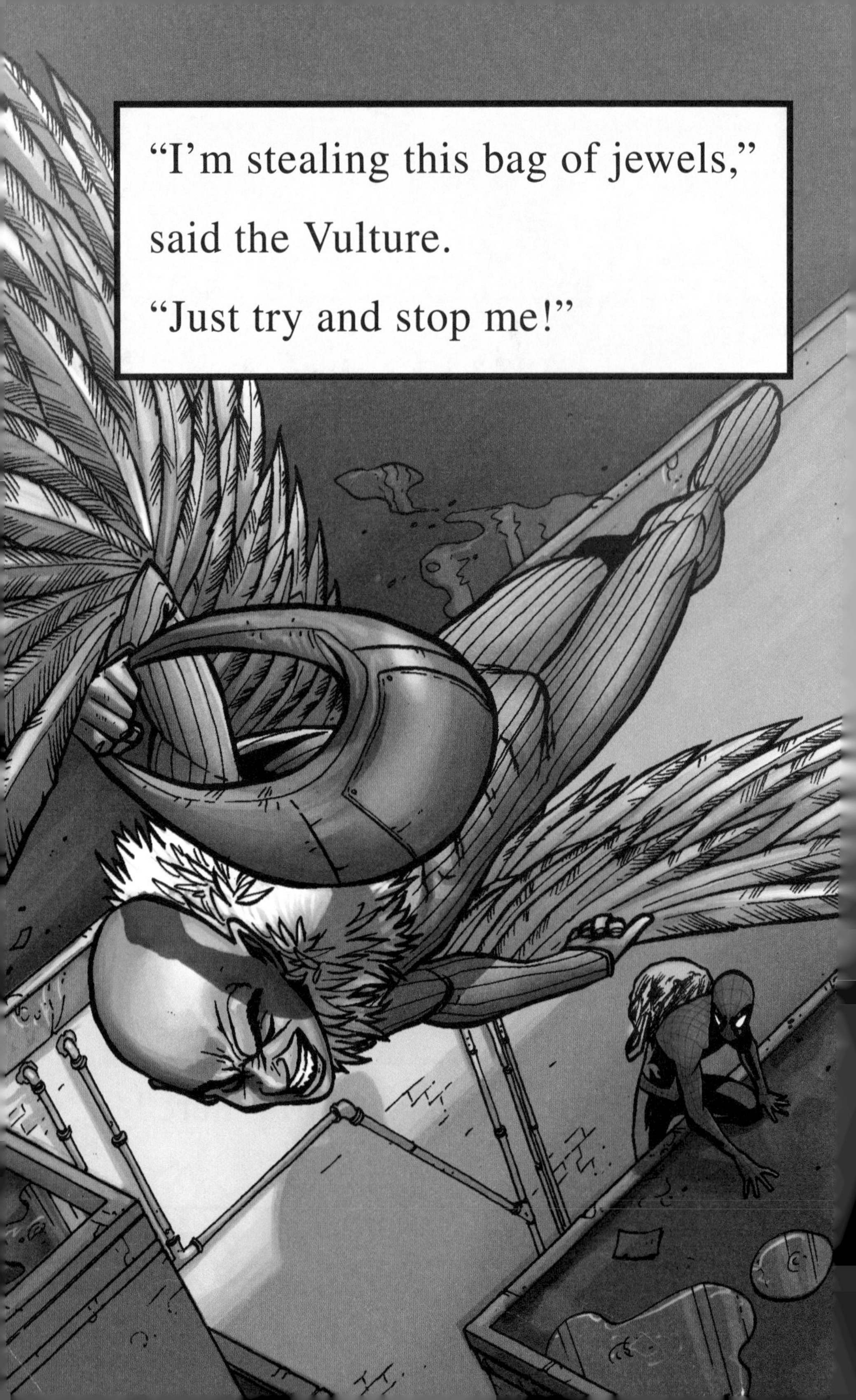

"I'm stealing this bag of jewels,"
said the Vulture.
"Just try and stop me!"

"Gosh," Spider-Man thought.

"I am so late.

I must get to the *Daily Bugle*."

Then Spidey remembered something.

With great power comes

great responsibility.

He had to stop the Vulture.

But where had the Vulture gone?

The Vulture swooped behind
Spider-Man on silent wings.
One flick of his wing
sent Spider-Man flying off the roof!

Spider-Man clung to the wall.

"How does Vulture fly

on silent wings?" he thought.

"I know! Silent magnetic power!"

Spider-Man climbed up the wall
on a web.

"I'm ready for you this time,
Vulture!" said Spider-Man.

Spider-Man took his homemade magnet reverser out of his backpack.

"This is the perfect time
to test my invention," he said.
Spider-Man aimed it at the Vulture.

"What did you do?
I can't fly!" said the Vulture.

The Vulture crashed to the ground.

"My invention worked!" said Spidey.

The police grabbed the Vulture.

Spider-Man snapped some pictures.

Click-click!

"My new boss will love these photos!"

he said.

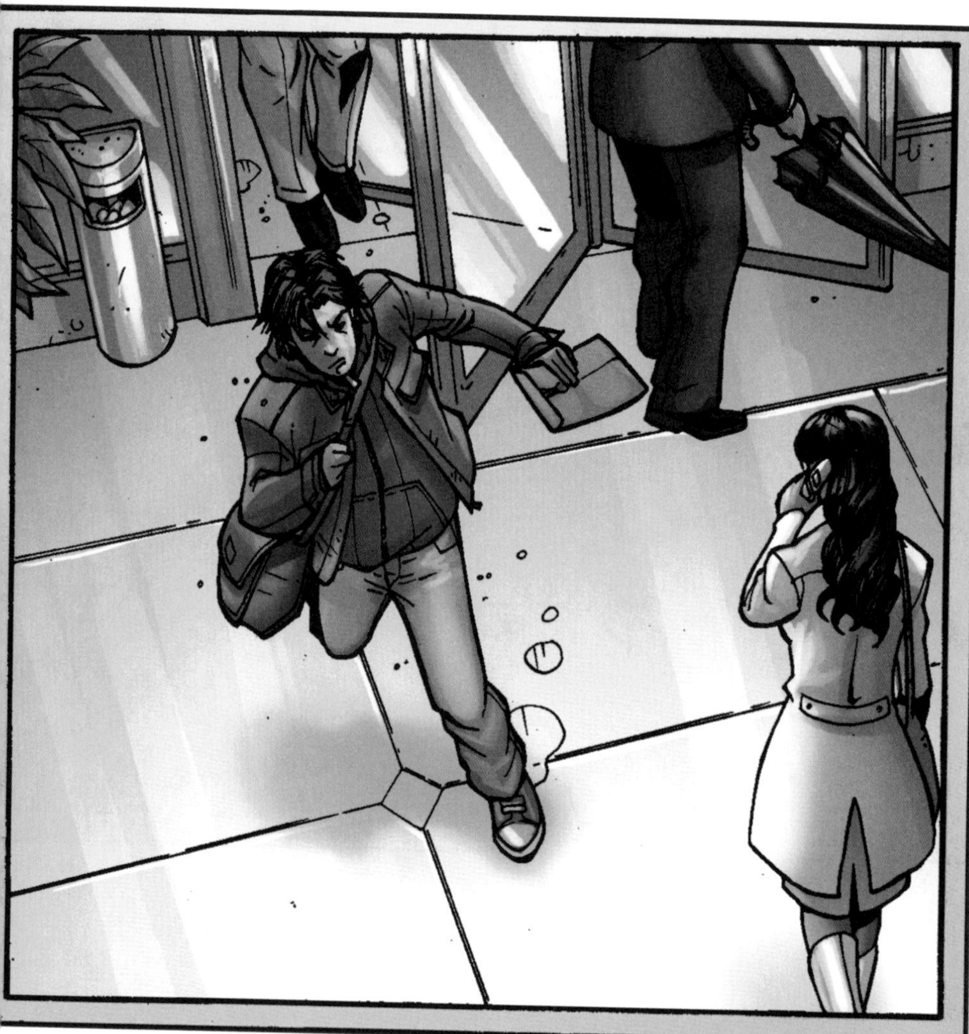

Peter put on his street clothes.

He was very late now.

He hurried to the *Daily Bugle*.

The boss, Mr. Jameson, was mad.

"Parker! You're late!" he yelled.

"But wait till you see my photos,"
said Peter.

"How did a shy guy like you get great photos like these?" said Mr. Jameson.

"All in a day's work," Peter said.

Mr. Jameson paid Peter well.

Now Peter could do something nice

for his aunt May.

Splash!

"Ha-ha! Sorry, nerd!" said Flash.

"If I used my amazing spider-powers, he really would be sorry!" thought Peter.

But Peter was happy,
even if no one could ever know
his amazing secret.

"I'm not a nerd. I'm Spider-Man!"

11/10